For Mrs. Boisvert's 2017-2018
third grade class, who were
our first critics

Mother Nature's Christmas Tree

Written by
Jennifer K. Armstrong
and
Illustrated by
Michelle Heiser

"Well, boys and girls, it's that time of year again. Mother Nature will soon choose her Christmas tree. Have you heard of Mother Nature? She cares for all of the earth's plants and animals.

She will travel deep into the forest to find the most perfect pine, special spruce, or flawless fir like she has done for centuries.

She'll place a gleaming star atop the chosen tree. Creatures near and far will come to marvel at her Christmas tree's majestic beauty."

"I'll be back in exactly one week to choose this year's Christmas tree," Mother Nature told the trees.

There was a loud rustling as the trees reacted with disbelief.

"Settle down, settle down," Mother Nature scolded. "I know one week isn't much time, but I have a very busy schedule."

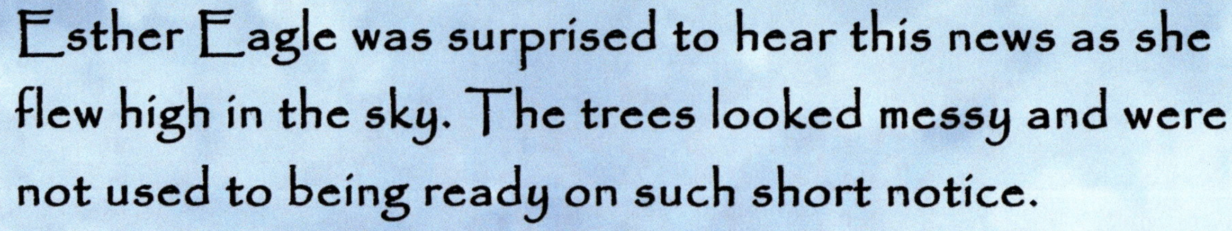

Esther Eagle was surprised to hear this news as she flew high in the sky. The trees looked messy and were not used to being ready on such short notice.

There's much to do, after all, to become a perfect Christmas tree. There's shearing and shaping, trimming and tapering, and of course, stretching and straightening.

One little pine, however, was not the least bit concerned.

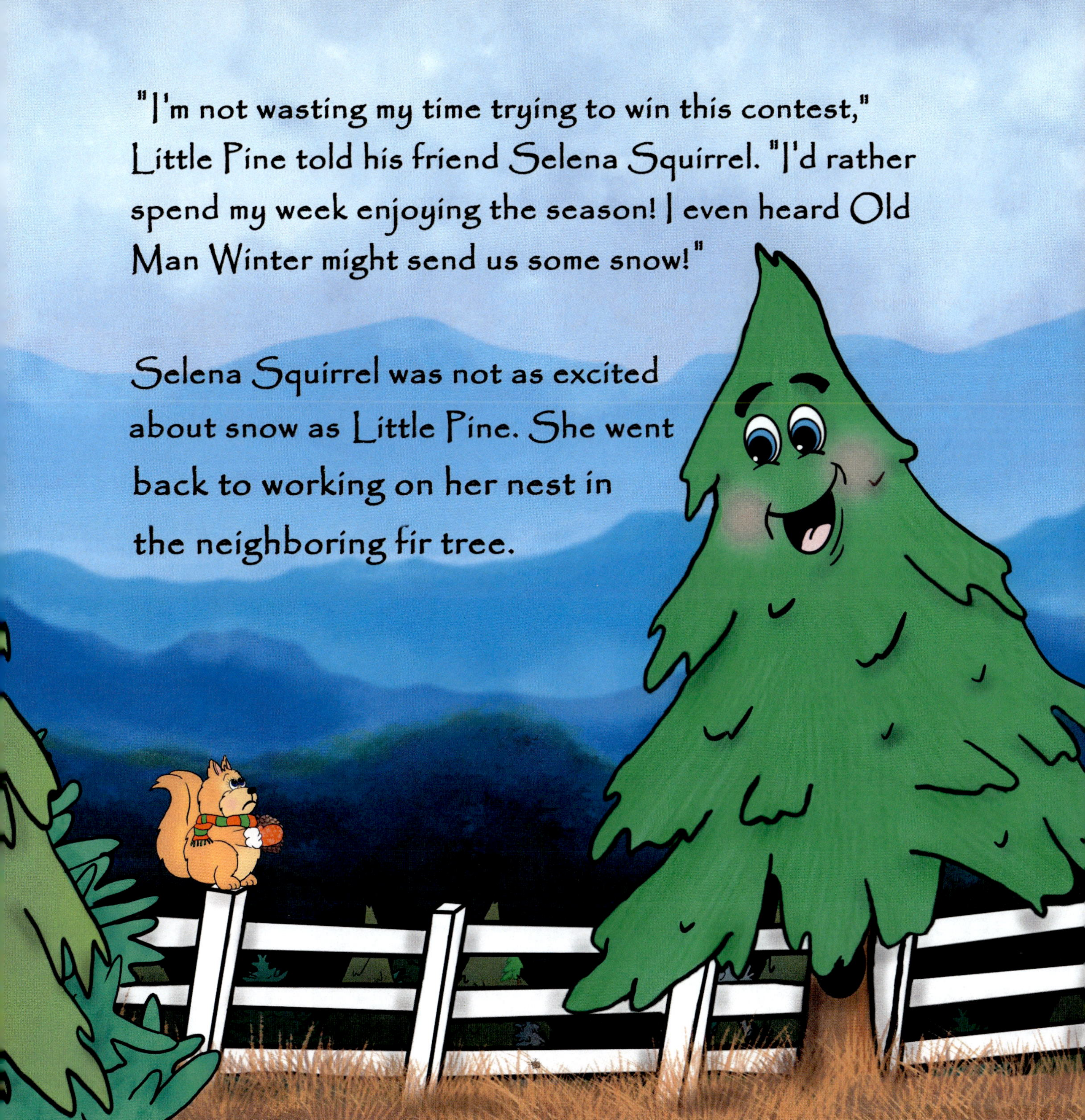

"I'm not wasting my time trying to win this contest," Little Pine told his friend Selena Squirrel. "I'd rather spend my week enjoying the season! I even heard Old Man Winter might send us some snow!"

Selena Squirrel was not as excited about snow as Little Pine. She went back to working on her nest in the neighboring fir tree.

Frilly Fir complained to Selena Squirrel, "I'm terribly sorry, little squirrel, but you need to find another place for your nest. Mother Nature is coming back in exactly one week and I need to be as clean and green as possible! Your squirrel's nest cannot clutter my flawless limbs."

Selena Squirrel didn't know what to do. She started to cry. After all, she and the squirrels she lived with needed a home to stay warm.

Later that day, as the sun disappeared behind the mountains, Little Pine had an idea. "Selena Squirrel, you can move your nest onto my limbs. I have pine cones you can eat. I'll give you shelter from the coming snow."

"Thank you, Little Pine. That is very gracious," chattered Selena Squirrel. "I'll round up my friends to help with the move."

Esther Eagle noticed Little Pine's graciousness as she flew high in the sky.

The following day, Spectacular Spruce gave a similar lecture to Momma Deer who bedded down beneath him.

"You're making a mess of me! My fallen needles have to lay sprinkled around my trunk for when Mother Nature returns. I can't have them pushed around to make a bed for you! You need to find another place to live," grumbled Spectacular Spruce.

Momma Deer didn't know what to do. She started to fret. After all, she and her fawns needed a home to stay warm.

"Don't worry, Momma Deer," Little Pine called out. "My fallen needles are soft and will give you a comfortable place to rest. My bark will make a good snack. You can move your family under my limbs and I'll give you shelter from the coming snow."

"Thank you, Little Pine, that is very kind," responded Momma Deer. "We'll move once my babies wake from their nap."

Esther Eagle noticed Little Pine's kindness as she flew high in the sky.

The following day was the same, as was the day after that. Deer, squirrels and even the black-capped chickadees could no longer live in the tall, strong, beautiful trees.

"Prissy Pine told me I have to move my nest," Miss Chickadee told her friend as they flew past Little Pine. "She said she needed to be clean and green and tall and straight because she dreamed of being Mother Nature's Christmas tree. She told me to vacate her trunk immediately! Oh, the nerve! Kicking out a sweet little bird like me in the cold of winter!"

"I didn't even make the hole in her trunk, I was just living in it! I'm going to freeze to death!" worried the little bird.

Miss Chickadee didn't know what to do. She started to panic. After all, she needed a home to stay warm.

Little Pine shouted to the passing bird, "Miss Chickadee, don't panic! I have a hole in my trunk from when Walter Woodpecker lived in it. You can roost there. I'll give you shelter from the coming snow."

Miss Chickadee landed on one of Little Pine's sturdy branches.

"Really?" she tweeted. "Thank you, Little Pine, thank you. You are very generous. I'll fly home and start moving. Prissy Pine can have her beautiful trunk, and I can have a warm, friendly place to live."

Esther Eagle noticed Little Pine's generosity as she flew high in the sky.

A northern spotted owl named Oscar was listening from a spruce nearby. He knew it wouldn't be long before Significant Spruce, who was last year's Christmas tree, would want him gone as well. He swooped over and landed gently on Little Pine. Little Pine's needles were long and soft.

Oscar Owl quietly hooted, "May I come live here too? You have been so welcoming to my forest friends. I know this will be a safe place for me to stay."

"Of course!" responded Little Pine. "You can huddle deep in my branches. I'll give you shelter from the coming snow."

Esther Eagle noticed Little Pine's hospitality as she flew high in the sky.

The next morning, Charly, a chubby mother chipmunk, scampered across the forest floor. Little Pine felt the familiar tickle as she scurried up his trunk.

"Little Pine, I just know I can count on you. Fabulous Fir told me she's really, really sorry that she has to ask me to find a different place to live until after Mother Nature chooses her tree. Fabulous Fir is working hard on being this year's Christmas tree. She doesn't like having holes around her roots where I go in and out of my burrow," Charly Chipmunk explained.

"I have no problem with holes around my roots. Just stay out of the deer family's way and I'll give you shelter from the coming snow," Little Pine told Charly Chipmunk.

"Thanks for helping me," Charly Chipmunk replied with relief. She started digging her new burrow; she didn't have much time. Mother Nature would be here soon.

Esther Eagle noticed Little Pine's helpfulness as she flew high in the sky.

The rest of that day, and the following day too, Little Pine showed love and compassion to animals who needed homes.

He was not concerned that his limbs were cluttered with nests, his pine needles were not evenly sprinkled on the ground, and there were holes around his roots.

Finally, it was the day of Mother Nature's arrival. Esther Eagle flew out to meet her at the edge of the forest. "Welcome back, Mother Nature! You're right on time!" she screeched as she landed on Matty Moose, who was pulling Mother Nature's carriage.

"Thank you, Esther! I am very excited to see the trees and to select my Christmas tree!" Mother Nature replied.

Esther Eagle had a lot to tell her, so she rode along as Mother Nature was carried deep into the forest.

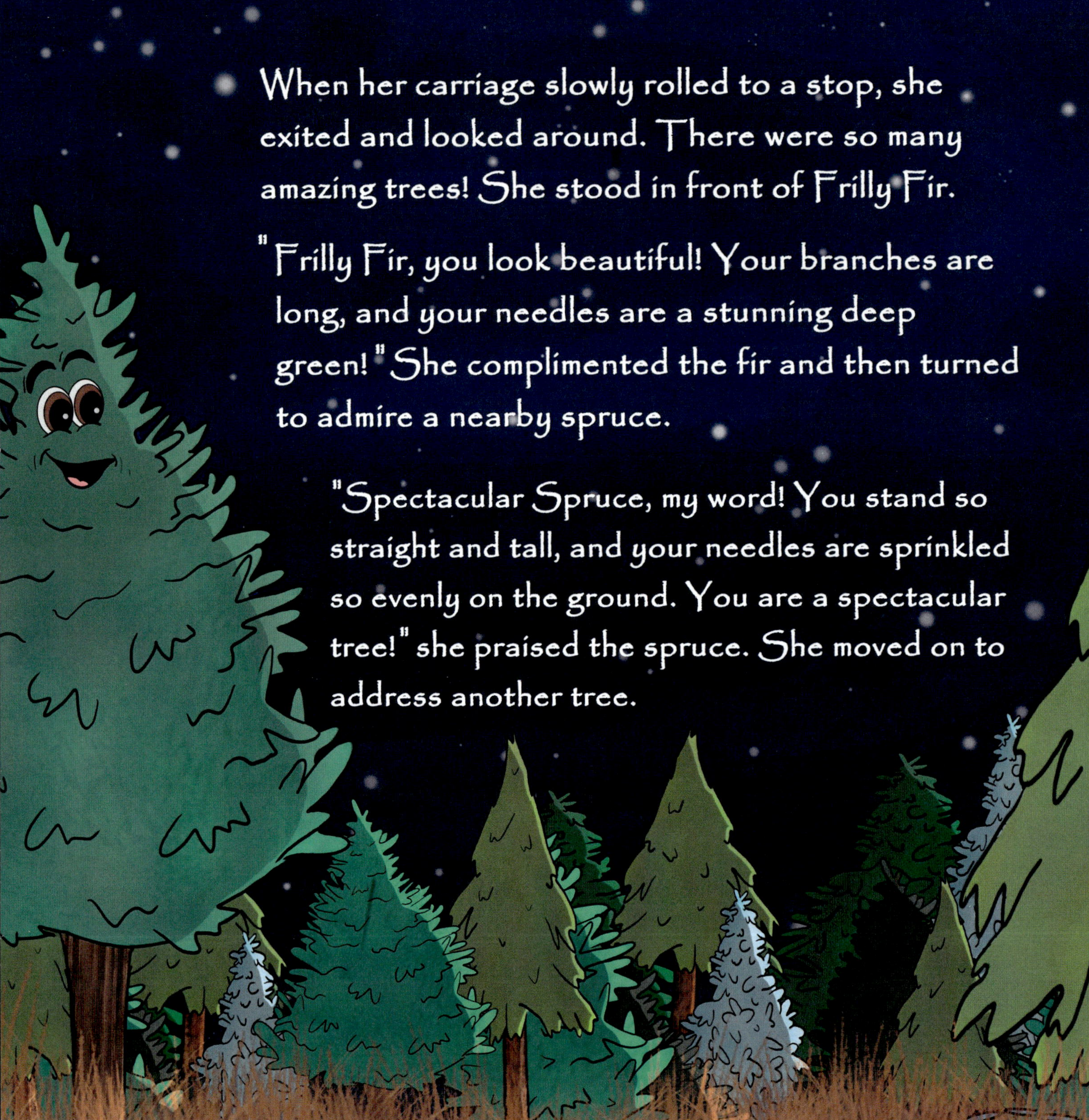

When her carriage slowly rolled to a stop, she exited and looked around. There were so many amazing trees! She stood in front of Frilly Fir.

"Frilly Fir, you look beautiful! Your branches are long, and your needles are a stunning deep green!" She complimented the fir and then turned to admire a nearby spruce.

"Spectacular Spruce, my word! You stand so straight and tall, and your needles are sprinkled so evenly on the ground. You are a spectacular tree!" she praised the spruce. She moved on to address another tree.

"Prissy Pine, I can tell you've worked hard to be chosen as this year's Christmas tree. You look so clean and green and tall and straight. You have all of the qualities of a perfect Christmas tree," admired Mother Nature.

She continued looking carefully at the trees until finally she came to Significant Spruce. "Oh, Significant Spruce! What a marvelous tree you are! I chose you last year for being so clean and green and tall and straight."

Mother Nature paused. The trees waited anxiously to see if Significant Spruce would again be chosen, but Mother Nature spun on her heels and walked over to Little Pine. She wasn't done.

"Little Pine, you are a mess," observed Mother Nature.

Little Pine felt uncomfortable as she continued.

"Nests clutter your limbs. Your pine needles aren't evenly sprinkled on the ground. You have holes in your trunk and around your roots."

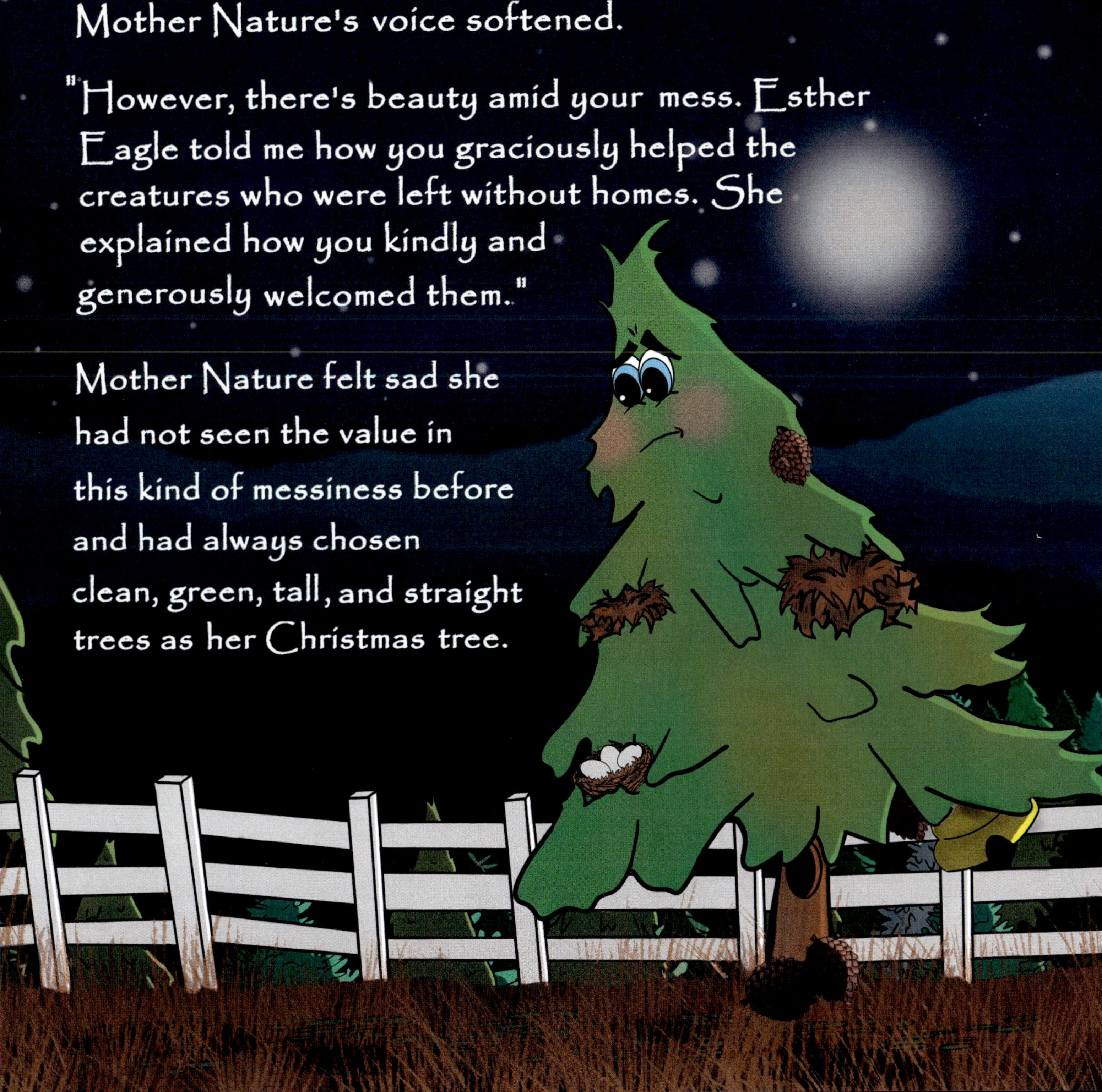

Mother Nature's voice softened.

"However, there's beauty amid your mess. Esther Eagle told me how you graciously helped the creatures who were left without homes. She explained how you kindly and generously welcomed them."

Mother Nature felt sad she had not seen the value in this kind of messiness before and had always chosen clean, green, tall, and straight trees as her Christmas tree.

This year would be different. This year she would choose Little Pine. She would send a message to all the forest about the importance of caring for the creatures who lived there.

"Little Pine, I'm choosing you as this year's Christmas tree," Mother Nature declared.

The trees were shocked. They listened silently as Mother Nature explained.

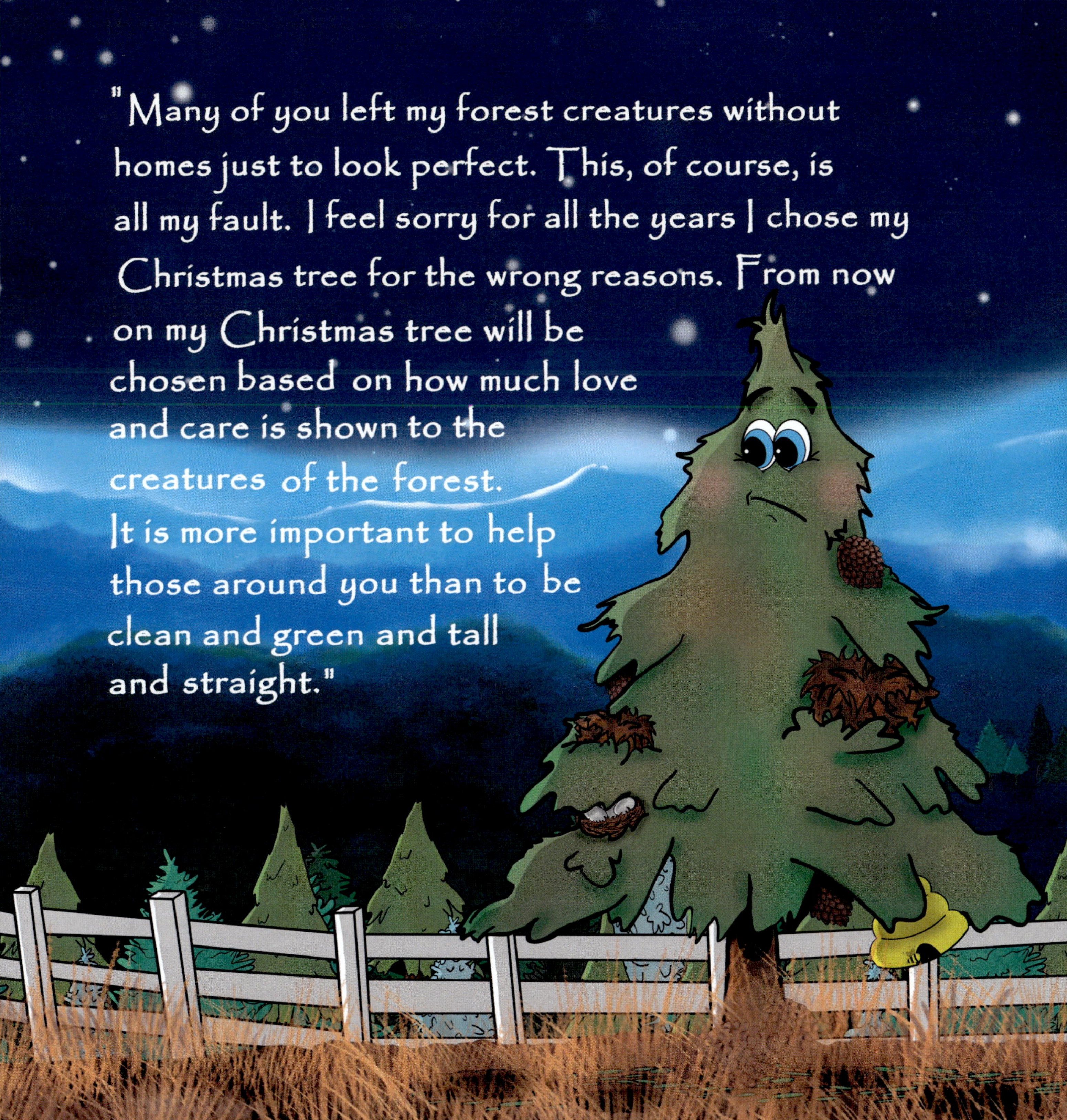

"Many of you left my forest creatures without homes just to look perfect. This, of course, is all my fault. I feel sorry for all the years I chose my Christmas tree for the wrong reasons. From now on my Christmas tree will be chosen based on how much love and care is shown to the creatures of the forest. It is more important to help those around you than to be clean and green and tall and straight."

"It was with these words, boys and girls, that Mother Nature placed her gleaming star atop Little Pine, naming him this year's Christmas tree. She was forever grateful for how Esther Eagle's keen eyesight helped her see that Little Pine *was* the perfect Christmas tree. Christmas, after all, is a time for giving generously and being kind and helpful to those in need, and that is just what Little Pine did."

Made in the USA
Monee, IL
30 October 2020

45530625R00024